LIBRARY SMARTS

SHARE YOUR BOOK REPORT

LISA OWINGS

Lerner Publications Company • Minneapolis

Lerner Publications Company
A division of Lerner Publishing Group, Inc.
241 First Avenue North
Minneapolis, MN 55401 U.S.A.

Website address: www.lernerbooks.com

Library of Congress Cataloging-in-Publication Data

Owings, Lisa.
    Share your book report / by Lisa Owings.
        pages cm. — (Library smarts)
    Includes index.
    ISBN 978–1–4677–1504–1 (lib. bdg. : alk. paper)
    ISBN 978–1–4677–1753–3 (eBook)
    1. Report writing—Juvenile literature. 2. Book reviewing—Juvenile
literature. I. Title.
LB1047.3.O95 2014
371.30281—dc23
                                      2013002303

Manufactured in the United States of America
1 – CG – 7/15/13

TABLE OF CONTENTS

Read a Book

Books can do wonderful things. They can teach you anything. They can show you other places and times. They can take you on adventures!

A book **report** can be wonderful too. It helps you think about a book. It helps you tell others about the book.

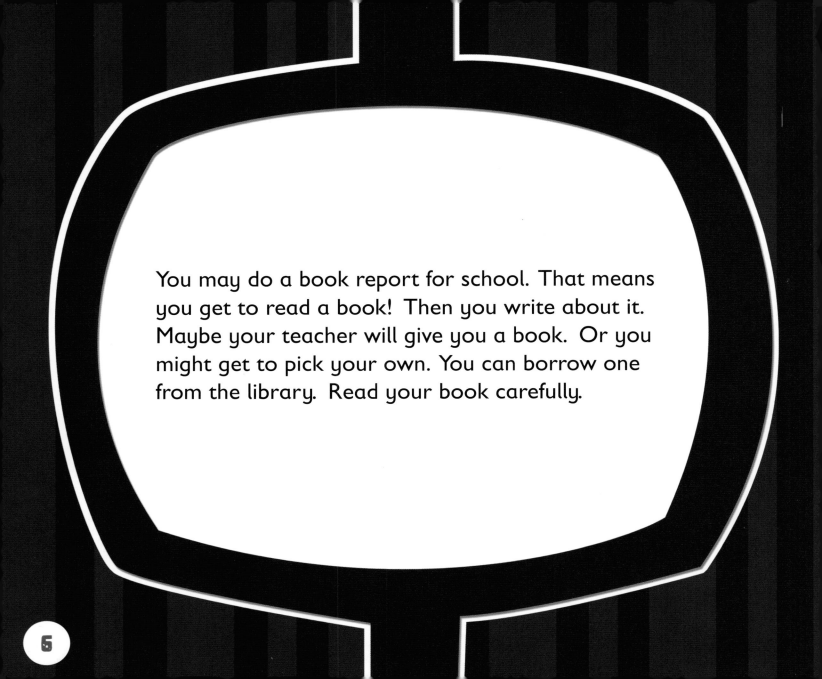

You may do a book report for school. That means you get to read a book! Then you write about it. Maybe your teacher will give you a book. Or you might get to pick your own. You can borrow one from the library. Read your book carefully.

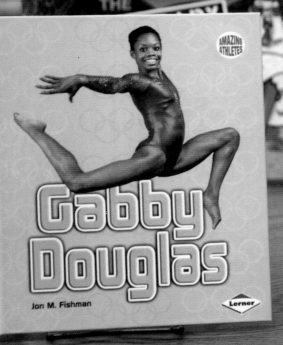

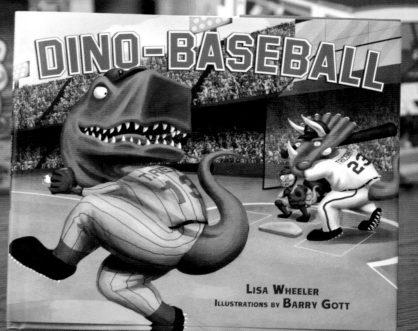

Write about Setting and Characters

Read all the way to the end of your book. Then start your book report. First, write your name on your paper. Then write the **title** of your book. Who wrote the book? That person is the **author**. What kind of book did you read? Was it true or made up? Write that down too.

Guess What Is Growing Inside This Egg

Title

Author

MIA POSADA

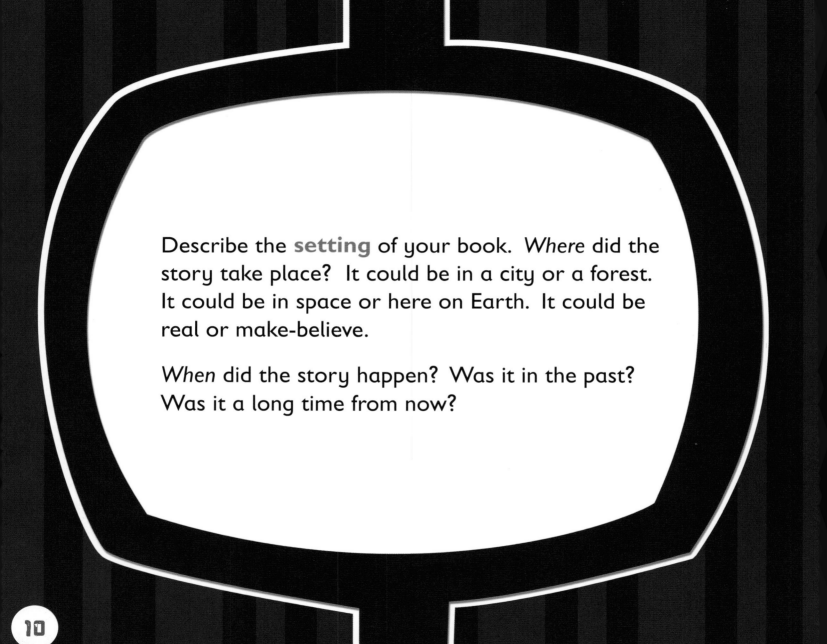

Describe the **setting** of your book. *Where* did the story take place? It could be in a city or a forest. It could be in space or here on Earth. It could be real or make-believe.

When did the story happen? Was it in the past? Was it a long time from now?

Most books have **characters**. They are often people or animals. But they can be other things too. Think about your book. Who were the important characters? Make a list. Write a few words about each one.

What Does a Screwdriver Do?
by Robin Nelson

Let's Make a Circle Graph
How Mr. Hall's Class Gets to School
by Robin Nelson

LIFE CYCLES
Apple Trees
by Robin Nelson

These are nonfiction books, or true books. Was your book true? Then you will write a different kind of report. Your teacher can help.

FROM Cocoa Bean TO Chocolate

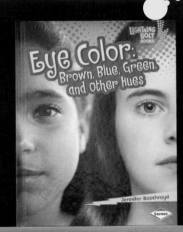
Eye Color: Brown, Blue, Green, and Other Hues
Jennifer Boothroyd

FROM Kernel TO Corn

Formula One Race Cars on the Move
Janet Piehl

FROM Egg TO Butterfly
Shannon Zemlicka

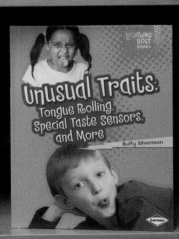
Unusual Traits: Tongue Rolling, Special Taste Sensors, and More
Buffy Silverman

Write about Plot and Ending

Writing about the plot is easy. Tell what happened in the story. Pretend you're talking to a friend. Your friend doesn't want to know everything that happened. Share only the important things. Start with the beginning. Then tell what happened in the middle. Was there a problem in the story?

Next, write about how your story ended. Think about the ending. Did it solve the problem? Was it a good ending? Tell why you think so.

Think about the whole book. What did you learn? Write your thoughts in your report.

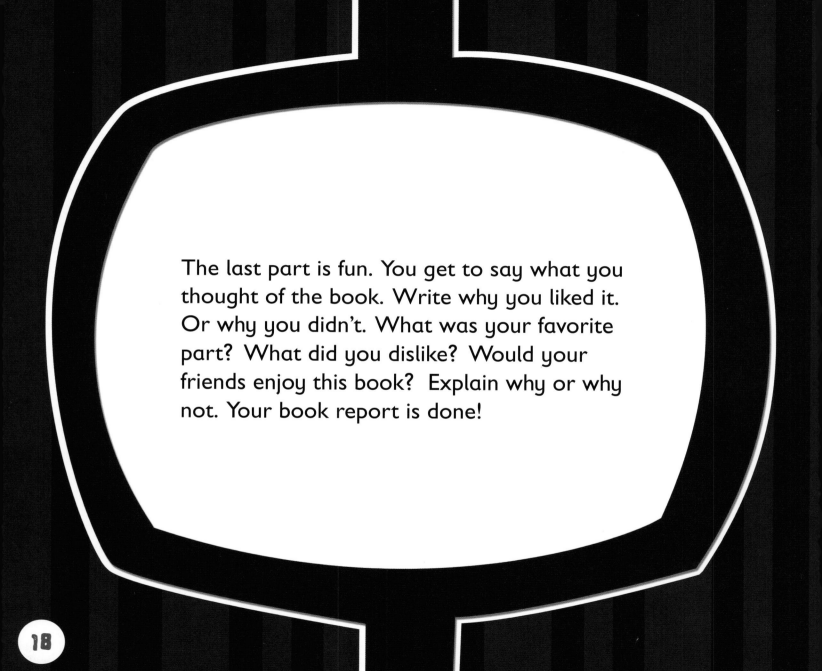

The last part is fun. You get to say what you thought of the book. Write why you liked it. Or why you didn't. What was your favorite part? What did you dislike? Would your friends enjoy this book? Explain why or why not. Your book report is done!

Share Your Book Report

You can share your book report. That lets others know about your book. Maybe they will read it too! There are many ways to share. Make a poster or a painting. Write a letter or draw a map. Make a movie or sing a song. Your teacher will help you decide how to share.

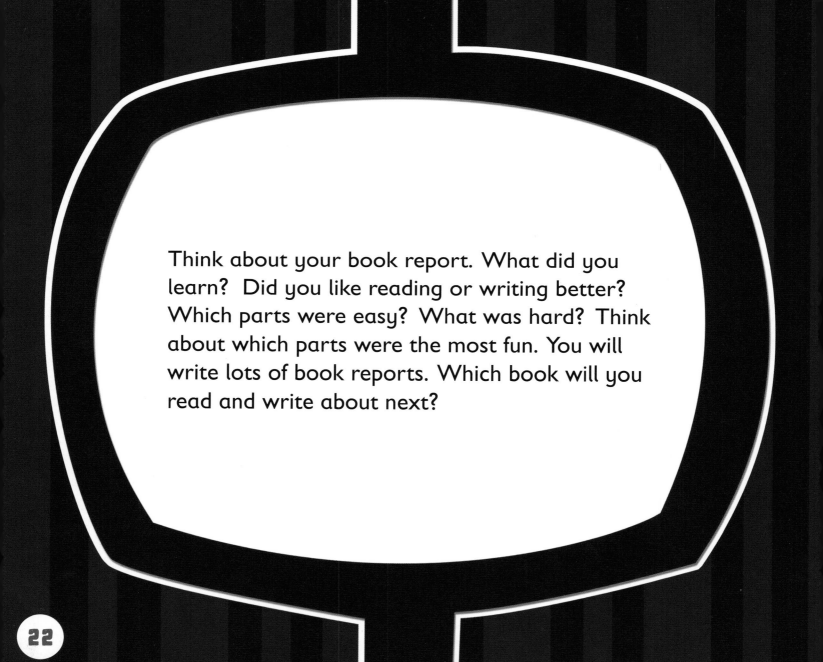

Think about your book report. What did you learn? Did you like reading or writing better? Which parts were easy? What was hard? Think about which parts were the most fun. You will write lots of book reports. Which book will you read and write about next?

GLOSSARY

author: the person who wrote a book

characters: people or animals in a story

plot: what happens in a story

report: words written about something. A book report is words written about one book.

setting: where and when a story takes place

title: the name of a book

INDEX

Photo acknowledgments: The images in this book are used with the permission of: © Monkey Business Images/Dreamstime.com, p. 5; © Todd Strand/Independent Picture Service, pp. 7, 9, 13, © Digital Vision/Photographer's Choice/Getty Images, p. 11; © Ilike/Shutterstock.com, p. 15; © Stockbyte Royalty Free, p. 17; © iStockphoto.com/laflor, p. 19; © iStockphoto.com/AVAVA, p. 21; © mattomedia Werbeagentur/Shutterstock.com, p. 23.

Front cover: © Tetra Images/Getty Images.

Main body text set in Gill Sans Infant Std Regular 18/22. Typeface provided by Monotype Typography.

nL   12-13